Giant Centipedes

by Grace Hansen

Abdo Kids Jumbo is an Imprint of Abdo Kids
abdobooks.com

abdobooks.com

Published by Abdo Kids, a division of ABDO, P.O. Box 398166, Minneapolis, Minnesota 55439.
Copyright © 2021 by Abdo Consulting Group, Inc. International copyrights reserved in all countries.
No part of this book may be reproduced in any form without written permission from the publisher.
Abdo Kids Jumbo™ is a trademark and logo of Abdo Kids.

Printed in the United States of America, North Mankato, Minnesota.

052020

092020

Photo Credits: Alamy, iStock, Science Source, Shutterstock

Production Contributors: Teddy Borth, Jennie Forsberg, Grace Hansen
Design Contributors: Dorothy Toth, Pakou Moua

Library of Congress Control Number: 2019956542
Publisher's Cataloging-in-Publication Data

Names: Hansen, Grace, author.

Title: Giant centipedes / by Grace Hansen

Description: Minneapolis, Minnesota : Abdo Kids, 2021 | Series: Spooky animals | Includes online resources
   and index.

Identifiers: ISBN 9781098202514 (lib. bdg.) | SBN 9781098203498 (ebook) | ISBN 9781098203986 (Read-
   to-Me ebook)

Subjects: LCSH: Centipedes--Juvenile literature. | Insects--Juvenile literature. | Insects--Behavior--Juvenile
   literature. | Curiosities and wonders--Juvenile literature.

Classification: DDC 596.018--dc23

Table of Contents

Giant Centipedes

Giant centipedes live in many places on Earth. There are many different species. But the largest of all lives in South America in the Amazon rain forest.

North America

Africa

Amazon
rain forest

South
America

This giant centipede has a long, flat body. It can grow to be 1 foot (30.48 cm) long!

More than 40 legs help it

scurry along the forest's floor.

Sometimes it even climbs

high up in trees.

The first pair of legs, behind its head, are claws. These claws are also called forcipules. They deliver deadly **venom** to **prey**.

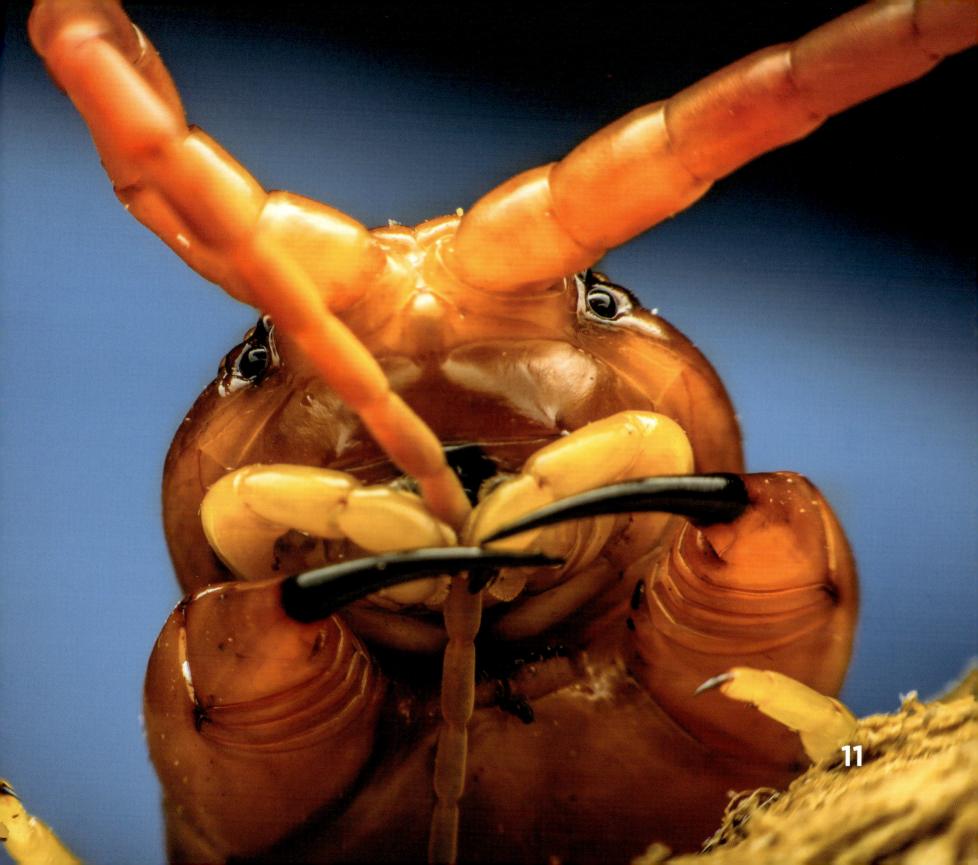

Hunting & Food

Giant centipedes hide in damp, dark places during the day. At night, they come out to hunt.

Giant centipedes are great hunters. They wrap their legs tightly around their prey. Then they pierce the animal with their forcipules.

Giant centipedes mainly eat insects and worms. But they also eat larger prey, like toads and mice. They have even been known to eat bats!

Baby Giant Centipedes

Female giant centipedes are caring mothers. They wrap their bodies around their eggs. This protects the eggs.

18

Newly hatched centipedes are called larvae. The larvae are born with all of their legs. Their mothers protect them. Soon they will be big enough to care for themselves.

21

More Facts

- A giant centipede's legs are made to quickly attack. They are also good for escaping danger.

- A giant centipede's **venom** can easily kill small **prey**.

- The venom is also toxic to humans. However, it is not likely to kill a human. But it will cause strong pain, swelling, and a fever.

Glossary

larva – an insect after it hatches from an egg and before it changes to its adult form.

prey – an animal that is hunted and eaten by another animal for food.

species – a group of living things that look alike and can have young with one another, but not with those of other groups.

venom – the poison that certain animals produce. It is put into prey by biting or stinging.

Index

Abdo Kids
ONLINE
FREE! ONLINE MULTIMEDIA RESOURCES

Visit **abdokids.com**
to access crafts, games,
videos, and more!

Use Abdo Kids code
SGK2514
or scan this QR code!